Mother Goose

A Random House PICTUREBACK®

MOTHER

GOOSE

ILLUSTRATED BY AURELIUS BATTAGLIA

 Random House New York

This title was originally catalogued by the Library of Congress as follows: Mother Goose. Mother Goose. Illustrated by Aurelius Battaglia. New York, Random House [1973] [32]p.: col. illus.; 21 cm. (A Random House Pictureback) SUMMARY: A selection of favorite Mother Goose rhymes. I. Nursery rhymes. [I. Nursery rhymes] I. Battaglia, Aurelius, illus. II. Title. PZ8.3.M85Bat5 398.8 73-2447 ISBN:0-394-83314-7 (B.C.); 0-394-82661-2 (trade); 0-394-92661-7 (lib. bdg.).

There was an old woman who lived in a shoe,
    She had so many children she didn't know what to do;
She gave them some broth, without any bread,
    And whipped them all soundly, and sent them to bed.

Ring-a-ring o' roses,
A pocket full of posies,
A-tishoo! A-tishoo!
We all fall down.

Jack, be nimble,
Jack, be quick,
Jack, jump over
The candlestick.

Pat-a-cake, pat-a-cake, baker's man,
Bake me a cake as fast as you can;

Pat it and prick it, and mark it with B,
And put it in the oven for Baby and me.

Jack Sprat could eat no fat,
   His wife could eat no lean,
And so between the two of them,
   They licked the platter clean.

Three little kittens,
They lost their mittens,
And they began to cry,
Oh, mother dear, we sadly fear
Our mittens we have lost.

What! Lost your mittens,
You naughty kittens!
Then you shall have no pie.
Mee-ow, mee-ow, mee-ow.
No, you shall have no pie.

The three little kittens,
They found their mittens,
And they began to cry,
Oh, mother dear, see here, see here,
Our mittens we have found.

Put on your mittens,
You silly kittens,
And you shall have some pie.
Purr-r, purr-r, purr-r,
Oh, let us have some pie.

The three little kittens
    Put on their mittens,
And soon ate up the pie;
Oh, mother dear, we greatly fear
Our mittens we have soiled.

What! Soiled your mittens,
    You naughty kittens!
Then they began to sigh,
Mee-ow, mee-ow, mee-ow.
Then they began to sigh.

The three little kittens,
    They washed their mittens,
And hung them out to dry;
Oh, mother dear, do you not hear
Our mittens we have washed?

What! Washed your mittens,
    Then you're good kittens!
But I smell a rat close by.
Mee-ow, mee-ow, mee-ow,
We smell a rat close by.

As I was going to St. Ives,
I met a man with seven wives;
Each wife had seven sacks,
Each sack had seven cats,
Each cat had seven kits;
Kits, cats, sacks, and wives,
How many were going to St. Ives?

Simple Simon met a pieman,
Going to the fair;

Says Simple Simon to the pieman,
Let me taste your ware.

Says the pieman to Simple Simon,
Show me first your penny;

Says Simple Simon to the pieman,
Indeed I have not any.

Hey diddle, diddle,
The cat and the fiddle,
The cow jumped over the moon;
The little dog laughed
To see such sport,
And the dish ran away with the spoon.

Pussy cat, pussy cat, where have you been?
I've been to London to look at the queen.
Pussy cat, pussy cat, what did you there?
I frightened a little mouse under her chair.

Old Mother Hubbard
Went to the cupboard
To fetch her poor dog a bone;

But when she came there
The cupboard was bare,
And so the poor dog had none.

She took a clean dish
To get him some tripe;
But when she came back
He was smoking a pipe.

She went to the grocer's
To buy him some fruit;
But when she came back
He was playing the flute.

She went to the baker's
To buy him some bread;
But when she came back
The poor dog was dead.

She went to the undertaker's
To buy him a coffin;
But when she came back
The poor dog was laughing.

She went to the hatter's
To buy him a hat;
But when she came back
He was feeding the cat.

The dame made a curtsey,
The dog made a bow;
The dame said, Your servant,
The dog said, Bow-wow.

Sing a song of sixpence,
A pocket full of rye;
Four and twenty blackbirds
Baked in a pie!

When the pie was opened,
The birds began to sing;
Wasn't that a dainty dish
To set before the king?

The king was in his counting-house,
  Counting out his money;
The queen was in the parlor,
  Eating bread and honey.

The maid was in the garden,
  Hanging out the clothes;
There came a little blackbird,
  And snapped off her nose.

This little pig went to market,

This little pig stayed home,

This little pig had roast beef,
This little pig had none,

And this little pig cried,
Wee-wee-wee-wee,
All the way home.

As I went to Bonner,
  I met a pig
  Without a wig,
Upon my word and honor.

Barber, barber, shave a pig,
How many hairs to make a wig?
Four and twenty, that's enough,
Give the barber a pinch of snuff.

Three young rats with black felt hats,
Three young ducks with white straw flats,
Three young dogs with curling tails,
Three young cats with demi-veils,

Went out to walk with two young pigs
In satin vests and sorrel wigs.
But suddenly it chanced to rain
And so they all went home again.

Rub-a-dub-dub,
   Three men in a tub,
And how do you think they got there?
   The butcher, the baker,
   The candlestick-maker,
   They all jumped out of a rotten potato,
'Twas enough to make a fish stare.

Georgie Porgie, pudding and pie,
Kissed the girls and made them cry;
When the boys came out to play,
Georgie Porgie ran away.

Cobbler, cobbler, mend my shoe,
Get it done by half-past two;
Half-past two is much too late,
Get it done by half-past eight.

There was a crooked man, and he walked a crooked mile,
He found a crooked sixpence against a crooked stile;
He bought a crooked cat, which caught a crooked mouse,
And they all lived together in a little crooked house.

Hark, hark,
  The dogs do bark,
The beggars are coming to town;
  Some in rags,
  And some in tags,
And one in a velvet gown.

Little Jack Horner
Sat in the corner,
  Eating a Christmas pie;
He put in his thumb,
And pulled out a plum,
And said, What a good boy am I!

Hickory, dickory, dock,
  The mouse ran up the clock;
  The clock struck one,
  The mouse ran down,
Hickory, dickory, dock.

I do not like thee, Doctor Fell,
The reason why I cannot tell;
But this I know, and know full well,
I do not like thee, Doctor Fell.

Goosey, goosey, gander!
  Where shall I wander?
Upstairs and downstairs,
And in my lady's chamber;
There I met an old man
Who would not say his prayers;
I took him by the left leg,
And threw him down the stairs.

Three blind mice, see how they run!
They all ran after the farmer's wife,
Who cut off their tails with a carving knife,

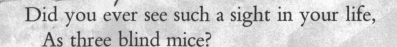

Did you ever see such a sight in your life,
  As three blind mice?

Taffy was a Welshman,
 Taffy was a thief;
Taffy came to my house
 And stole a piece of beef.

I went to Taffy's house,
 Taffy was not home;
Taffy came to my house
 And stole a mutton bone.

I went to Taffy's house,
 Taffy was not in;
Taffy came to my house
 And stole a silver pin.

I went to Taffy's house,
 Taffy was in bed;
I took up a poker
 And threw it at his head.

Yankee Doodle came to town,
  Riding on a pony;
He stuck a feather in his hat
  And called it macaroni.

Old King Cole
 Was a merry old soul,
And a merry old soul was he;
 He called for his pipe,
 And he called for his bowl,
And he called for his fiddlers three.

Humpty Dumpty
Sat on a wall,

Humpty Dumpty
Had a great fall,

All the king's horses and all the king's men,
Couldn't put Humpty together again.

Doctor Foster went to Gloucester
In a shower of rain;
He stepped in a puddle,
Right up to his middle,
And never went there again.

Star light, star bright,
First star I see tonight,
I wish I may, I wish I might,
Have the wish I wish tonight.